青蛙和蟾蜍
好朋友
Frog and Toad Are Friends

文／圖　艾諾·洛貝爾 *Arnold Lobel*

譯　潘人木　黨英台

我會讀系列 中英雙語

⊙上誼

Frog and Toad Are Friends (bilingual edition)

Copyright © 1970 by Arnold Lobel

Published by arrangement with Harper & Row, Publishers, Inc.,

New York, N. Y., U. S. A.

Chinese Text © HSINEX INTERNATIONAL CORPORATION 1989

中文版授權 上誼文化實業股份有限公司

青蛙和蟾蜍───好朋友 (中英雙語)

文、圖／艾諾‧洛貝爾 譯／黨英台 譯文審定者／潘人木

總策畫／張杏如 總編輯／高明美 企劃／溫碧珠、邱孟嫻

執行編輯／郭恩惠 美術編輯／廖瑞文、林勵勳 生產管理／王彥森

發行人／張杏如 出版／上誼文化實業股份有限公司 地址／台北市重慶南路二段75號

電話／(02)23913384(代表號) 網址／http://www.hsin-yi.org.tw

郵撥／10424361 上誼文化實業股份有限公司 定價／(書＋英文 CD)220 元

2001年6月初版 2014年1月初版十四刷 ISBN／957-762-246-1

印刷／中華彩色印刷股份有限公司

有版權‧勿翻印 如有破損或裝訂錯誤請寄回更換 讀者服務／信誼‧奇蜜親子網 www.kimy.com.tw

目　次

Contents

春天到了

青蛙加快腳步，
跑上通往蟾蜍家的小路。
到了蟾蜍家，
他敲敲門，
沒有人答應。
「蟾蜍，蟾蜍，」
青蛙大聲的叫：
「快點起床，春天到了！」
「瞎扯，」
屋子裡傳來一個
模糊的聲音。
「蟾蜍！蟾蜍！」
青蛙又喊：

4

「太陽出來了，
雪在融化了，
你該醒來了。」
「我不在家。」那個聲音說。

青蛙自己開了門，
走進蟾蜍的小屋。
裡面一片黑乎乎。
所有的窗戶都關著，
所有的窗簾都垂著。
「蟾蜍，你在哪兒啊？」
青蛙叫著。
「走開！」那個聲音
從屋子的一角傳來。

青蛙一看，
蟾蜍還躺在床上，
被子蒙到頭上了。
青蛙把蟾蜍推下床。
又推出臥房，
推到了門外的走廊。
外面的太陽好明亮，
晃得蟾蜍直眨眼。
他說：「救命啊！
我什麼也看不見了。」

「別傻了，」青蛙說：
「你看見了
四月明亮溫暖的陽光。
這也就是說，
我們可以開始一起度過
這新的一年了，蟾蜍。」
青蛙又說：
「你想想看，那該多好啊，
我們可以在草地上蹦跳，
在樹林裡奔跑，
還可以在小河裡游泳。
到了夜晚，
我們就坐在這兒，
數著天上的星星。」
「要數星星你去數吧，青蛙，
我可沒這個興致。」
蟾蜍說：

「這會兒
我要回房睡覺去了。」

蟾蜍轉身回到屋子裡，
跳上床， 拉起被子，
又要蒙頭大睡。
「 可是， 蟾蜍， 」
青蛙著急了：
「 你會錯過
一大堆好玩的事情！ 」
「 那你告訴我， 」蟾蜍說：
「 我到底睡了多久啦？ 」

「你呀，打從去年十一月就一直睡，
睡到現在了。」青蛙回答。
「這麼說，我再多睡
一小會兒，也不要緊。」
蟾蜍說：「等過了五月半，
你再回來，把我叫醒好了。
再見，青蛙。」

「可是，蟾蜍，」青蛙說：
「這樣一來，
我就會孤孤單單的，
一直到那個時候啊！」
蟾蜍沒吭聲，
他已經睡著了。
青蛙看看蟾蜍的月曆，
十一月的那張還在上面。
青蛙把十一月的那張撕掉，

又撕掉了十二月的那張，
一月的那張，
二月的那張，
三月的那張，
撕到了四月的那張。
青蛙把四月的那張
也撕掉了。

青蛙跑到蟾蜍的床邊。

「蟾蜍，蟾蜍，快起來，
現在是五月了。」

「什麼？」蟾蜍說：

「五月這麼快就到了？」

「是啊，」青蛙說：

「不信，看看你的月曆嘛。」

蟾蜍看看月曆，
五月的那張果然在最上面。

「哇！真的是五月了！」
蟾蜍說著，
一骨碌爬下床。
然後，
他和青蛙跑到外面去，
看看春天的大地
是個什麼樣兒。

講故事

夏季裡有一天，
青蛙覺得身體
有點兒不舒服。
蟾蜍說：「青蛙，
你的臉色有點發綠喔。」
青蛙說：
「我一直都是綠綠的，
我是一隻青蛙啊。」
蟾蜍說：「就算是一隻青蛙，
你今天的臉色也未免
太綠了一點兒。
快到我的床上躺下來，
休息休息。」
蟾蜍給青蛙
泡了一杯熱茶。

青蛙喝了茶，說：
「我在這兒休息，
你講個故事給我聽吧。」

「好的。」蟾蜍說：
「我來想想看。」
蟾蜍想啊想啊，
可就是想不出一個故事
來講給青蛙聽。

18

「 我到門廊那兒走一走，」
蟾蜍說：
「 這樣也許我就能
想出個故事來。 」
蟾蜍走到門廊那兒，
來來回回的走了好久。
可就是想不出一個故事
來講給青蛙聽。

然後蟾蜍回到屋子裡，
頭朝下倒立著。
青蛙看了問：
「你幹嘛在那兒倒立著？」
蟾蜍說：
「我希望這樣倒立著，
能使我想出個故事來。」

蟾蜍倒立了好久，
還是想不出一個故事
來講給青蛙聽。

21

然後蟾蜍拿來一杯水，
潑在自己的頭上。

青蛙問：

「你幹嘛往自己的頭上
潑水呢？」

蟾蜍說：

「我希望往頭上潑點水，
能使我想出個故事來。」

蟾蜍接連往自己的頭上
潑了好幾杯水。

還是想不出個故事

來講給青蛙聽。

然後，蟾蜍
又用頭往牆
上砰砰的撞。
青蛙問：
「你幹嘛用頭去撞牆呢？」
蟾蜍說：「我希望把我的頭
往牆上狠狠的撞，
能讓我想出個故事來。」

青蛙說：
「我這會兒覺得好多了，
我不想聽什麼故事了。」
蟾蜍說：
「那你起來，
讓我躺一下吧。
我現在覺得很不舒服。」
青蛙說：「蟾蜍，要不要
我來講個故事給你聽呢？」
「好啊，」 蟾蜍說：
「你有故事就講吧。」

青蛙說：

「從前有兩個好朋友，

一個是青蛙，

一個是蟾蜍。

有一天，

青蛙有點不舒服。

他要求他的好朋友蟾蜍

講個故事給他聽。

蟾蜍想不出什麼故事。

他到門廊那兒走來走去，

可就是想不出個故事來。

他把頭朝下倒立著，

也想不出個故事來。

他往頭上潑水，

也想不出個故事來。

他又用頭去撞牆，

還是想不出個故事來。

結果青蛙好了，
蟾蜍反倒病了。
所以蟾蜍上床去休息，
青蛙起來，
給蟾蜍講了一個故事。
講完了，蟾蜍，
這個故事好聽嗎？」
但是蟾蜍沒有回答，
他已經睡著了。

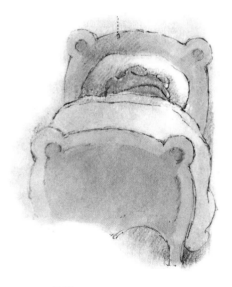

一顆遺失的扣子

青蛙和蟾蜍一起去散步。
他們走了好長的一段路。
他們穿過大草地，
他們走進樹林裡。
他們沿著河邊走啊走的，
最後他們回到了
蟾蜍的家。
「真倒霉！」蟾蜍說：
「這一趟不但把我的腿
走痠了，
外套上的扣子
也走掉了一顆。」

青蛙說：「別擔心，
我們可以順著
剛才走過的路，
回頭去找啊，
很快就會找到
你那顆扣子的。」
他們回到大草地。
開始在深深的草叢裡
找那顆扣子。

「找到了！你的扣子
在這兒哪！」青蛙大聲叫著。
「這不是我的扣子，」
蟾蜍說：
「我的扣子是白色的，
這顆扣子是黑色的。」
蟾蜍把這顆黑色的扣子
放進口袋裡。

一隻麻雀飛下來，他說：
「請問，你們是不是
丟了一顆扣子？
我這兒撿到了一顆。」
「這不是我的扣子，」
蟾蜍說：
「我的扣子有四個洞，
這顆扣子有兩個洞。」
蟾蜍把這顆兩個洞的扣子
放進口袋裡。

他們回到樹林裡，
低著頭，
在陰暗的小路上
找啊找的。
「找到了！你的扣子
在這兒哪！」青蛙說。
「這不是我的扣子，」
蟾蜍大聲的叫著：
「我的扣子是顆大扣子，
這是顆小扣子。」
蟾蜍又把這顆小扣子
放進口袋裡。

一隻浣熊從
一棵大樹後面出來，
他說：
「聽說你們在找一顆扣子，
喏， 這兒有一顆，
是我剛才撿到的。」
「這才不是我的扣子呢，」
蟾蜍傷心的說：
「我的扣子是圓的，
這顆扣子是方的。」
蟾蜍又把這顆方扣子
放進口袋裡。

青蛙和蟾蜍走回河邊，
在岸上的泥巴裡找啊找的。
「找到了，你的扣子
在這兒哪！」青蛙說。
「這才不是我的扣子呢！」
蟾蜍大聲的喊：
「我的扣子是厚厚的，
這顆扣子是薄薄的。」

蟾蜍又把這顆薄薄的
扣子放進口袋裡。
他好生氣啊。
他上上下下的跳著，
大聲的尖叫著：
「這個世界上
到處都是扣子，
卻沒有一顆是我的！」
蟾蜍氣呼呼的跑回家，

把門狠狠的一關。
你猜怎麼樣，
他看見那顆白色的，
有四個洞的，
又大又厚的圓扣子
就在地板上呢。
「啊！」蟾蜍說：
「原來它一直是在這兒，
我卻給青蛙找了
多少麻煩哪。」

蟾蜍把口袋裡所有的
扣子都拿出來，
又從架子上拿來針線盒。
他把那些扣子
這裡一顆那裡一顆的，
都縫在他的外套上了。

第二天，

蟾蜍把他的外套送給青蛙。

青蛙覺得它好漂亮。

他穿上這件外套，

高興得跳了起來。

上面的扣子

卻一顆也沒有掉，

因為蟾蜍把它們縫得

很牢很牢。

那天他們去游泳

蟾蜍和青蛙
走到小河邊。
青蛙說：
「好一個游泳天！」
「是啊！」 蟾蜍說：
「我要到這堆石頭後面
換游泳衣去。」
青蛙說：
「我是不穿游泳衣的。」
「你不穿， 我可要穿。」
蟾蜍說：
「待會兒我穿上游泳衣，
可不許你看喲，

要ㄧㄠˋ等ㄉㄥˇ到ㄉㄠˋ我ㄨㄛˇ下ㄒㄧㄚˋ水ㄕㄨㄟˇ以ㄧˇ後ㄏㄡˋ
才ㄘㄞˊ能ㄋㄥˊ看ㄎㄢˋ。」

「爲什麼不許我看呢？」
青蛙問。

「因爲我穿上游泳衣的
樣子很滑稽，
就爲這個啦。」蟾蜍說。
蟾蜍從石頭後面
走出來的時候，
青蛙還閉著眼睛，
蟾蜍已經換上游泳衣了。

「別偷看喔，」他說。

青蛙和蟾蜍跳進水裡，

他們游了整整一個下午。

青蛙游得快，

水花濺得高；

蟾蜍游得慢，

水花濺得小。

一隻烏龜來到河邊。

蟾蜍說：「青蛙，

你去叫那隻烏龜走開。

等一會兒

我上岸的時候，

不想讓他看到

我穿游泳衣的樣子。」

青蛙游到烏龜那兒去，

他說：

「烏龜，你得走開。」

「我爲什麼要走開？」

烏龜問。

「因爲蟾蜍認爲他穿
游泳衣的樣子很滑稽，
不想讓你看見他。」

青蛙說。

45

幾隻蜥蜴坐在附近，
他們齊聲的問：
「蟾蜍穿游泳衣的樣子
真的很滑稽嗎？」
一條蛇從草叢裡爬出來，
他說：「要是蟾蜍
穿游泳衣的樣子
真的很滑稽，
我倒想看看。」

「我們也想看看。」
兩隻蜻蜓說。

「我也要看，」
一隻田鼠說：
「我好久都沒看見什麼
滑稽可笑的東西了。」

青蛙游回蟾蜍那兒，說：
「對不起，蟾蜍，
每個人都要看你穿
游泳衣的樣子呢。」
蟾蜍說：「既然這樣，
我只好一直待在水裡，
等他們走開再說了。」
烏龜、蜥蜴、蛇、蜻蜓
和田鼠都坐在河邊。
他們等著蟾蜍從水裡出來。
「拜託啦！」
青蛙大聲的喊：
「拜託各位走開啦！」
可是沒有一個走開的。
蟾蜍在水裡越待越冷。
他開始渾身發抖又打噴嚏。

「我得出去了。」蟾蜍說：
「這樣下去我會感冒的。」

蟾蜍從河裡爬上岸，
游泳衣上的水，
滴滴答答的
落在他的腳上。
烏龜看了哈哈大笑。

蜥ㄒㄧ蜴ㄧˋ看ㄎㄢˋ了ㄌㄜ˙哈ㄏㄚ哈ㄏㄚ大ㄉㄚˋ笑ㄒㄧㄠˋ。

蛇ㄕㄜˊ看ㄎㄢˋ了ㄌㄜ˙哈ㄏㄚ哈ㄏㄚ大ㄉㄚˋ笑ㄒㄧㄠˋ。

田ㄊㄧㄢˊ鼠ㄕㄨˇ看ㄎㄢˋ了ㄌㄜ˙哈ㄏㄚ哈ㄏㄚ大ㄉㄚˋ笑ㄒㄧㄠˋ。

青ㄑㄧㄥ蛙ㄨㄚ看ㄎㄢˋ了ㄌㄜ˙也ㄧㄝˇ哈ㄏㄚ哈ㄏㄚ大ㄉㄚˋ笑ㄒㄧㄠˋ。

蟾蜍說：

「青蛙，你笑什麼？」

「我在笑你呀，蟾蜍，」

青蛙說：

「因為你穿游泳衣的

樣子，**確實**很滑稽。」

「本來就是嘛！」

蟾蜍說。

然後他撿起自己的衣服

回家了。

等信

蟾蜍坐在走廊上。
青蛙走過來，說：
「怎麼啦，蟾蜍？
你看起來
很傷心的樣子。」

「是啊，」蟾蜍說：
「這是我每天的
傷心時刻。
我天天在這個時候等信，
結果總是叫我很掃興。」
「怎麼會呢？」青蛙問。
「因為我從來沒接到過
一封信。」蟾蜍說。
「從來沒接到過嗎？」
青蛙問。

「沒有，從來沒有。」
蟾蜍說：
「從來就沒有一個人
寫信給我。
我的信箱每天都是空的。
所以等信的時間，
就成了我的傷心時間。」
青蛙和蟾蜍坐在走廊上，
一同傷心難過。

過了一會兒，青蛙說：
「我現在得回家一趟，
有件事我要回去做。」
青蛙急急忙忙回到家裡。

他找出一枝鉛筆
和一張信紙。
他在信紙上寫了一些字。

他把信紙放進一個信封裡。

在信封上，他寫著：

「 給蟾蜍的信 」

青蛙拿著這封信

跑到屋子外邊，

看見了熟朋友蝸牛。

青蛙說：

「 蝸牛啊，拜託你把

這封信送到蟾蜍家，

放在他的信箱裡。 」

「 好吧， 」 蝸牛說：

「 我這就去。 」

然後，　青蛙跑回蟾蜍家。
蟾蜍躺在床上，
正在那兒睡午覺呢。
「蟾蜍，」　青蛙說：
「我看你還是起來，
再多等一會兒送信的吧。」
「算了，」　蟾蜍說：
「我等信等得煩透了。」

58

青蛙望望窗外
蟾蜍的信箱。
蝸牛還沒有到。
「蟾蜍，」青蛙說：
「說不定有人會
寄信給你呢。」
「不可能，不可能的，」
蟾蜍說：
「絕對不會有人
寄信給我的。」

青蛙又望望窗外，
蝸牛還沒有到。
「可是，蟾蜍呀，」
青蛙說：
「也許今天就有人
寄信給你喲。」
「別傻了，」蟾蜍說：
「以前從來沒有人
寄信給我，
今天也不會有人
寄信給我。」

青蛙望望窗外，
蝸牛還是沒到。
蟾蜍問：「青蛙，
你為什麼老是往窗外看？」
青蛙說：「因為我在
等信哪。」
「不會有信的啦。」
蟾蜍說。

「會有，一定會有。」
青蛙說：

「因為我寄了
一封信給你。」

「你寄了嗎？」　蟾蜍問：

「你在信上
寫了些什麼呀？」
青蛙說：

「我是這樣寫的：

『　親愛的蟾蜍，　我很高興
你是我最好的朋友。
你最好的朋友青蛙上。　』」
「　啊，　」　蟾蜍說：
「　這封信寫得好棒喔！　」
於是青蛙和蟾蜍走出去，
一同到門廊那兒去等信。
他們坐在那兒，
心裡都很快樂。

青蛙和蟾蜍等了
好久好久。
四天以後，
蝸牛總算到了蟾蜍的家，
把青蛙寫的信交給蟾蜍。
蟾蜍接到信，
高興極了。

64

Spring

Frog ran up the path to Toad's house.

He knocked on the front door.

There was no answer.

"Toad, Toad," shouted Frog,

"wake up. It is spring!"

"Blah," said a voice

from inside the house.

"Toad! Toad!" cried Frog.

"The sun is shining!

The snow is melting. Wake up!"

"I am not here," said the voice.

Frog walked into the house.

It was dark.

All the shutters were closed.

"Toad, where are you?" called Frog.

"Go away," said the voice
from a corner of the room.

Toad was lying in bed.
He had pulled all the covers over his head.
Frog pushed Toad out of bed.
He pushed him out of the house
and onto the front porch.
Toad blinked in the bright sun.
"Help!" said Toad.
"I cannot see anything."

"Don't be silly," said Frog.
"What you see
is the clear warm light of April.
And it means that we can begin
a whole new year together, Toad.
Think of it," said Frog.
"We will skip through the meadows
and run through the woods
and swim in the river.

In the evenings we will sit right here
on this front porch and count the stars."
"You can count them, frog," said Toad.
"I will be too tired.

I am going back to bed."

Toad went back into the house.
He got into the bed
and pulled the covers over his head again.
"But, Toad," cried Frog,
"you will miss all the fun!"
"Listen, Frog," said Toad.
"How long have I been asleep?"

"You have been asleep since November,"
said Frog.
"Well then," said Toad,
"a little more sleep will not hurt me.
Come back again and wake me up
at about half past May.

Good night, Frog."

"But, Toad," said Frog,
"I will be lonely until then."
Toad did not answer.
He had fallen asleep.
Frog looked at Toad's calendar.
The November page was still on top.
Frog tore off the November page.

He tore off the December page.
And the January page,
the February page,
and the March page.
He came to the April page.
Frog tore off the April page too.

Then Frog ran back to Toad's bed.
"Toad, Toad, wake up. It is May now."
"What ?" said Toad.
"Can it be May so soon?"

"Yes," said Frog.

"Look at your calendar."

Toad looked at the calendar.

The May page was on top.

"Why, it *is* May!" said Toad
as he climbed out of bed.
Then he and Frog ran outside
to see how the world was looking
in the spring.

The Story

One day in summer
Frog was not feeling well.
Toad said, "Frog,
you are looking quite green."
"But I always look green," said Frog.
"I am a frog."
"Today you look very green
even for a frog," said Toad.
"Get into my bed and rest."
Toad made Frog a cup of hot tea.

Frog drank the tea, and then he said,
"Tell me a story while I am resting."

"All right," said Toad.
"Let me think of a story to tell you."
Toad thought and thought.
But he could not think of a story to tell Frog.

"I will go out on the front porch
and walk up and down," said Toad.
"Perhaps that will help me
to think of a story."
Toad walked up and down
on the porch for a long time.
But he could not think of a story
to tell Frog.

Then Toad went into the house
and stood on his head.
"Why are you standing on your head?"
asked Frog.
"I hope that if I stand on my head,
it will help me to think of a story,"
said Toad.

Toad stood on his head for a long time.
But he could not think of a story
to tell Frog.

Then Toad poured a glass of water
over his head.
"Why are you pouring water
over your head?" asked Frog.
"I hope that if I pour water over my head,
it will help me to think of a story,"
said Toad.
Toad poured many glasses of water
over his head.
But he could not think of a story
to tell Frog.

Then Toad began to bang his head
against the wall.
"Why are you banging your head
against the wall?" asked Frog.
"I hope that if I bang my head
against the wall hard enough,
it will help me to think of a story,"
said Toad.

"I am feeling much better now, Toad,"
said Frog. "I do not think
I need a story anymore."
"Then you get out of bed
and let me get into it," said Toad,
"because now I feel terrible."
Frog said, "Would you like me
to tell you a story, Toad?"
"Yes," said Toad,
"if you know one."

"Once upon a time," said Frog,
"there were two good friends,
a frog and a toad.
The frog was not feeling well.
He asked his friend the toad
to tell him a story.
The toad could not think of a story.
He walked up and down on the porch,
but he could not think of a story.

He stood on his head,
but he could not think of a story.
He poured water over his head,
but he could not think of a story.
He banged his head against the wall,
but he still could not think of a story.

Then the toad did not feel so well,
and the frog was feeling better.
So the toad went to bed
and the frog got up and told him a story.
The end.
How was that, Toad?" said Frog.
But Toad did not answer.
He had fallen asleep.

A Lost Button

Toad and Frog went for a long walk.
They walked across a large meadow.
They walked in the woods.
They walked along the river.
At last they went back home to Toad's house.
"Oh, drat," said Toad.
"Not only do my feet hurt,
but I have lost
one of the buttons on my jacket."

"Don't worry," said Frog.
"We will go back to all the places
where we walked.
We will soon find your button."
They walked back to the large meadow.
They began to look for the button
in the tall grass.

"Here is your button!" cried Frog.

"That is not my button," said Toad.

"That button is black. My button was white."

Toad put the black button in his pocket.

A sparrow flew down.

"Excuse me," said the sparrow.

"Did you lost a button? I found one."

"That is not my button," said Toad.

"That button has two holes.

My button had four holes."

Toad put the button with two holes
in his pocket.

They went back to the woods
and looked on the dark paths.

"Here is your button," said Frog.

"That is not my button," cried Toad.

"That button is small. My button was big."

Toad put the small button in his pocket.

A raccoon came out from behind a tree.
"I heard that you were looking for a button,"
he said. "Here is one that I just found."
"That is not my button!" wailed Toad.
"That button is square.
My button was round."
Toad put the square button in his pocket.

Frog and Toad went back to the river.
They looked for the button in the mud.
"Here is your button," said Frog.
"That is not my button!" shouted Toad.
"That button is thin. My button was thick."

Toad put the thin button in his pocket.
He was very angry.
He jumped up and down and screamed,
"The whole world is covered with buttons,
and not one of them is mine!"
Toad ran home

and slammed the door.
There, on the floor, he saw his white,
four-holed, big, round, thick button.
"Oh," said Toad. "It was here all the time.
what a lot of trouble
I have made for Frog."

Toad took all of the buttons
out of his pocket.
He took his sewing box down from the shelf.
Toad sewed the buttons all over his jacket.

The next day Toad gave his jacket to Frog.
Frog thought that it was beautiful.
He put it on and jumped for joy.
None of the buttons fell off.
Toad had sewed them on very well.

A Swim

Toad and Frog went down to the river.

"What a day for a swim," said Frog.

"Yes," said Toad.

"I will go behind these rocks

and put on my bathing suit."

"I don't wear a bathing suit," said Frog.

"Well, I do," said Toad.

"After I put on my bathing suit,

you must not look at me

until I get into the water."

"Why not?" asked frog.

"Because I look funny in my bathing suit.

That is why," said Toad.

Frog closed his eyes when Toad came out

from behind the rocks.

Toad was wearing his bathing suit.

"Don't peek," he said.

Frog and Toad jumped into the water.

They swam all afternoon.

Frog swam fast and made big splashes.

Toad swam slowly

and made smaller splashes.

A turtle came along the riverbank.

"Frog, tell that turtle to go away,"

said Toad. "I do not want him to see me

in my bathing suit

when I come out of the river."

Frog swam over to the turtle.

"Turtle," said Frog,

"you will have to go away."

"Why should I?" asked the turtle.

"Because Toad thinks that

he looks funny in his bathing suit,

and he does not want you to see him,"

said Frog.

Some lizards were sitting nearby.
"Does Toad really look funny
in his bathing suit?" they asked.
A snake crawled out of the grass.
"If Toad looks funny in his bathing suit,"
said the snake,
"then I, for one, want to see him."

"We want to see him too,"
said two dragonflies.
"Me too," said a field mouse.
"I have not seen anything funny
in a long time."

Frog swam back to Toad.
"I am sorry, Toad," he said.
"Everyone wants to see
how you will look."
"Then I will stay right here
until they go away," said Toad.

The turtle and the lizards
and the snake and the dragonflies
and the field mouse
all sat on the riverbank.
They waited for Toad
to come out of the water.
"Please," cried Frog, "please go away!"
But no one went away.
Toad was getting colder and colder.
He was beginning to shiver and sneeze.

"I will have to come out of the water,"
said Toad. "I am catching a cold."

Toad climbed out of the river.
The water dripped out of his bathing suit
and down onto his feet.
The turtle laughed.

The lizards laughed.
The snake laughed.
The field mouse laughed,
and Frog laughed.

"What are you laughing at, Frog?"
said Toad.
"I am laughing at you, Toad," said Frog,
"because you *do* look funny
in your bathing suit."
"Of course I do," said Toad.
Then he picked up his clothes
and went home.

The Letter

Toad was sitting on his front porch.
Frog came along and said,
"What is the matter, Toad?
You are looking sad."

"Yes," said Toad.
"This is my sad time of day.
It is the time
when I wait for the mail to come.
It always makes me very unhappy."
"Why is that?" asked Frog.
"Because I never get any mail," said Toad.
"Not ever?" asked Frog.

"No, never," said Toad.
"No one has ever sent me a letter.
Every day my mailbox is empty.

That is why waiting for the mail
is a sad time for me."
Frog and Toad sat on the porch,
feeling sad together.

Then Frog said, "I have to go home now,
Toad. There is something that I must do."
Frog hurried home.
He found a pencil and a piece of paper.
He wrote on the paper.

He put the paper in an envelope.
On the envelope he wrote
"A LETTER FOR TOAD."
Frog ran out of his house.
He saw a snail that he knew.
"Snail," said Frog,
"Please take this letter to Toad's house
and put it in his mailbox."
"Sure," said the snail. "Right away."

Then Frog ran back to Toad's house.
Toad was in bed, taking a nap.
"Toad," said Frog,
"I think you should get up
and wait for the mail some more."
"No," said Toad,
"I am tired of waiting for the mail."

Frog looked out of the window
at Toad's mailbox.
The snail was not there yet.
"Toad," said Frog, "you never know
when someone may send you a letter."
"No, no," said Toad. "I do not think
anyone will ever send me a letter."

Frog looked out of the window.
The snail was not there yet.
"But, Toad," said Frog,
"someone may send you a letter today."
"Don't be silly," said Toad.

"No one has ever sent me a letter before,
and no one will send me a letter today."

Frog looked out of the window.
The snail was still not there.
"Frog, why do you keep looking
out of the window?" asked Toad.
"Because now I am waiting for the mail,"
said Frog.
"But there will not be any," said Toad.

"Oh, yes there will," said Frog,
"because I have sent you a letter."
"You have?" said Toad.
"What did you write in the letter?"
Frog said, "I wrote

'Dear Toad, I am glad that
you are my best friend.
Your best friend, Frog.'"

"Oh," said Toad,
"that makes a very good letter."
Then Frog and Toad went out
onto the front porch to wait for the mail.
They sat there, feeling happy together.

Frog and Toad waited a long time.
Four days later the snail got to Toad's house
and gave him the letter from Frog.
Toad was very pleased to have it.